Hello, Beautiful You

What to do with this book:
Speak it. Sing It. Bring it.
Shout it. Share it.

How to read this treasury:
Joyfully. Lovingly.
Again and again and again.

Where to savor this collection:
Inside. Outside. Crib Side.
Pillow Side. Stroller Side.

When to delight in these stories:
When your Bright Brown Baby is in your
arms. When you and your baby play.
Whenever the spirit moves you!

Who is this book for?
Every baby of every hue, from every
family who wants to Treasure You.

Bright Brown Baby

A TREASURY

by **Andrea Davis Pinkney** ✱ illustrated by **Brian Pinkney**

ORCHARD BOOKS
an imprint of Scholastic Inc. • New York

Welcome to Joy!

This book is a **Treasury**. And a **Treasure You**. And a **Treasure We**.

Yes, yes, yes — get ready for sweet togetherness. The time has come to cuddle on up with your little one. The moment has arrived to read, sing, celebrate. The day is here to let the Bright Brown Babies in your life know how truly special they are.

As you embrace these pages, here's an important fact: Reading aloud is good for a child's health. In the same ways air, food, and sunshine make babies grow strong and happy, so do books. And, like a day of bright skies, and a night that sparkles with stars, this book is our gift to you and every baby whose eyes are filled with tomorrow's promise.

PLEASE NOTE: As you read . . . hold your baby. Show your baby. Really get to know your Bright Brown precious child. The time has come to give that baby the stories and pictures that will hug them tight.

A final word about health. While reading this book with a child, you may experience any of the following side-effects: Intense feelings of joy. A miraculous sense of well-being. Overwhelming love. Expect these emotions to last a lifetime.

— Andrea & Brian Pinkney

The night is beautiful.
So the faces of my people.
The stars are beautiful,
So the eyes of my people.
Beautiful, also, is the sun.
Beautiful, also, are the souls
of my people.

— Langston Hughes

Bright Brown Baby

✴

Poet **Langston Hughes** expressed it wonderfully.

The faces, eyes, and souls of Black people are beautiful.

Now it's your turn.

Go on, **say it loud. Speak it proudly.**

Rejoice in the honest-to-goodness.

Tell all the Black and Brown children you meet how truly

extraordinary they are!

**Brown baby,
born bright.
Greet the world.
Spread your light.**

Sparkling eyes
blink hello.
Bright Brown Baby,
you will go . . .

Up, over,
around, and through.
Child, we believe
in you.

Bright Brown Baby,
yes we do.

Little one,
future bright.
**Brown baby,
alright!**

I have decided to stick with love.

— Martin Luther King, Jr.

Count to Love

✷

Get ready to make a big list of blessings.
Begin by telling your **Bright Brown Baby** what you've always
known: **"When I count my blessings, I count you twice."**
Go ahead, add them all up. Count the many gifts in your life,
starting with the little one who will share this book with you.
It all adds up to the words expressed through the wisdom of
Dr. Martin Luther King, Jr. By counting to love, blessings multiply.

Count to love on fingers and toes.

Count to love.
Two legs. Two arms.

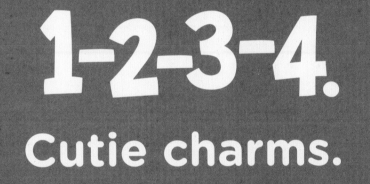

1-2-3-4.

Cutie charms.

Count to love
with belly kisses.

1-2-3-4.

Making wishes.

Count to love.
Wide eyes to see.

L-O-V-E,
you and me!

**Look to this day,
for it is life.**

— Ancient Sanskrit poem

Peek
-a-
YoU!

✴

Set your **sights** on your baby's eyes.

And **nose**.

And **lips**.

And beautiful **skin**.

Don't ever look away from the pretty possibilities that fill

that **Bright Brown** face.

Ancient wisdom puts it simply.

Today is the day.

Morning, nap time, mealtime, fun time — any time is a

good time to rejoice.

Turn the page to play a happy game of eyes-on-the-prize.

The reward? **Your baby's gaze!**

Peek-a-you,
peek-a-you,
take a look.

Peek-a-you,
peek-a-you,
in this book.

Peek-a-you,
peek-a-you,
stomp! Shout! Sing!

I am just the cutest thing.

peek-a-you, peek-a-you,
can you see?

Here's the pretty
brown face of **ME!**

Peek-a-WHO?

Baby, it's YOU!

Never let anyone...
diminish your light...
— Congressman John Lewis

Baby Boy, You Are a Star!

✴

Bright **Brown baby boys** are beautiful.
Bright Brown baby boys are brilliant.
Bright Brown baby boys are the legacy of all-things-special.
Bright Brown baby boys are sparkling lights born from a galaxy of greatness.

Tell them every chance you can. Plant these affirmations from the very first moment they come blinking into this world.

Yes, yes, cultivate these seeds of truth so your Brown boy takes hold. Don't let anything uproot his power. Remind him he's part of something **big**, **bold**, **important**, and **enduring**.

As he grows, he'll be your feisty little guy. The words of Congressman John Lewis remind us that to cultivate any boy's birthright, we need to let his light shine.

Tiny, bubbly bundle.
Blanket filled with joy.

Baby born,
darling one.
Sweetest
little boy.

Promise for tomorrow.

Child reaching far.

Baby boy.
Precious boy.

Yes!
You're a STAR!

Choose people who
lift you up.
— Michelle Obama

Hey, Baby Girl!

*

Be **the one** who reminds your girl she is preciousness personified!

Make no mistake. First Lady Michelle Obama reminds us to pick the people who help us shine.

Start right now, this minute, filling your child with **confidence**, **determination**, and a big dose of **yes-you-can**.

As your little lady grows, she'll be quick to let others know that shared wings help us all rise together.

Hey, baby girl.
Welcome to the world!

Baby girl eyes. See it.
Baby girl ears. Hear it.

Baby girl heart.
Beat it.

Baby girl smarts.

Read it.

You're the one, baby girl.

See.

Hear.

Beat.

Read.

Hey, baby girl.
Go change the world.

Celebrations of Color

Becoming parents has been the greatest gift of our lives. Our own Bright Brown Babies, Chloe and Dobbin, now grown, are the inspirations for the words and paintings in this book. Our daughter and son were each born with glistening skin. Their complexions were cause for celebration. Because, from the moment each drew their first breath, we instilled in them the understanding that their Blackness is truly beautiful.

That's because the books we read together showed babies who looked like themselves, bright and brown.

And now we invite you to join us in our ongoing celebration of children of color.

It starts with the pictures on the pages we share with our newborns. Because the truth of the matter is, babies see what they see, and they don't see what we don't show them. This Bright Brown Baby Treasury, and the accompanying board books that illuminate each individual title, say to babies: Beauty begins with you.

Now that you've enjoyed this collection, please go back and consider the words of the notable people that open each story. Read them slowly, and aloud, to your child. These are simple truths that will touch even the youngest minds and souls. Then, take another good look at the images that help tell the story of each narrative. Look at the shapes, colors, and play-swirls of joy. These represent energetic hearts, arms enfolding, hugs, love. With gouache and acrylic paints, and India ink on watercolor paper, the families of many complexions, shown in each vignette, celebrate bundles of Black and Brown joy, the wonders of curiosity and play, the precious affection that every child needs to know they are loved.

— Andrea & Brian Pinkney

To Beautiful Brown Babies everywhere!
— A.D.P. and B.P.

Library of Congress Cataloging-in-Publication Data available
Photos ©: Shutterstock.com
ISBN 978-0-545-87229-4
10 9 8 7 6 5 4 3 2 1   21 22 23 24 25
Printed in China   38
First edition, October 2021